Ricardo Demi

Where have you been,

little MAX?

Dear reader!

This is the second book in the Little Max series.
I hope you find it interesting and useful!

Kids love short stories with beautiful illustrations! They turn into real discoveries!

Discoveries help our little explorers learn about the world!

Knowledge of the world helps them develop and achieve great results!

This is true Magic!

With respect and best wishes,
Ricardo Demi

This book
belongs to

_____

_____

There is a mouse named Little Max who lives in a little town. He is kind and cheerful, and he loves to learn everything new and interesting. He also likes to tell stories.

Look, there he is running along the path!

Let's ask him:
"Where have you been, Little Max?"

I went to the zoo!

What is a zoo?

The zoo is a large home for many different animals, where you can visit them.

What animals did you see at the zoo, Little Max?

I saw a Lion with a big mane! He is the king of the animals and can roar loudly, like this: "Grr-r." It wasn't scary at all, and I also roared like a lion: "Grr-r."

I saw a Giraffe! He is very tall and has a long neck. A giraffe can reach the top of any tree. To greet him, I had to climb a ladder. Can you imagine?! And the Giraffe is kind and friendly, too!

I saw an Elephant and a Baby Elephant. The Elephant is the largest animal in the zoo. He has a long trunk and large ears. He can use his trunk to do different jobs and even take a shower. And I made friends with the Baby Elephant!

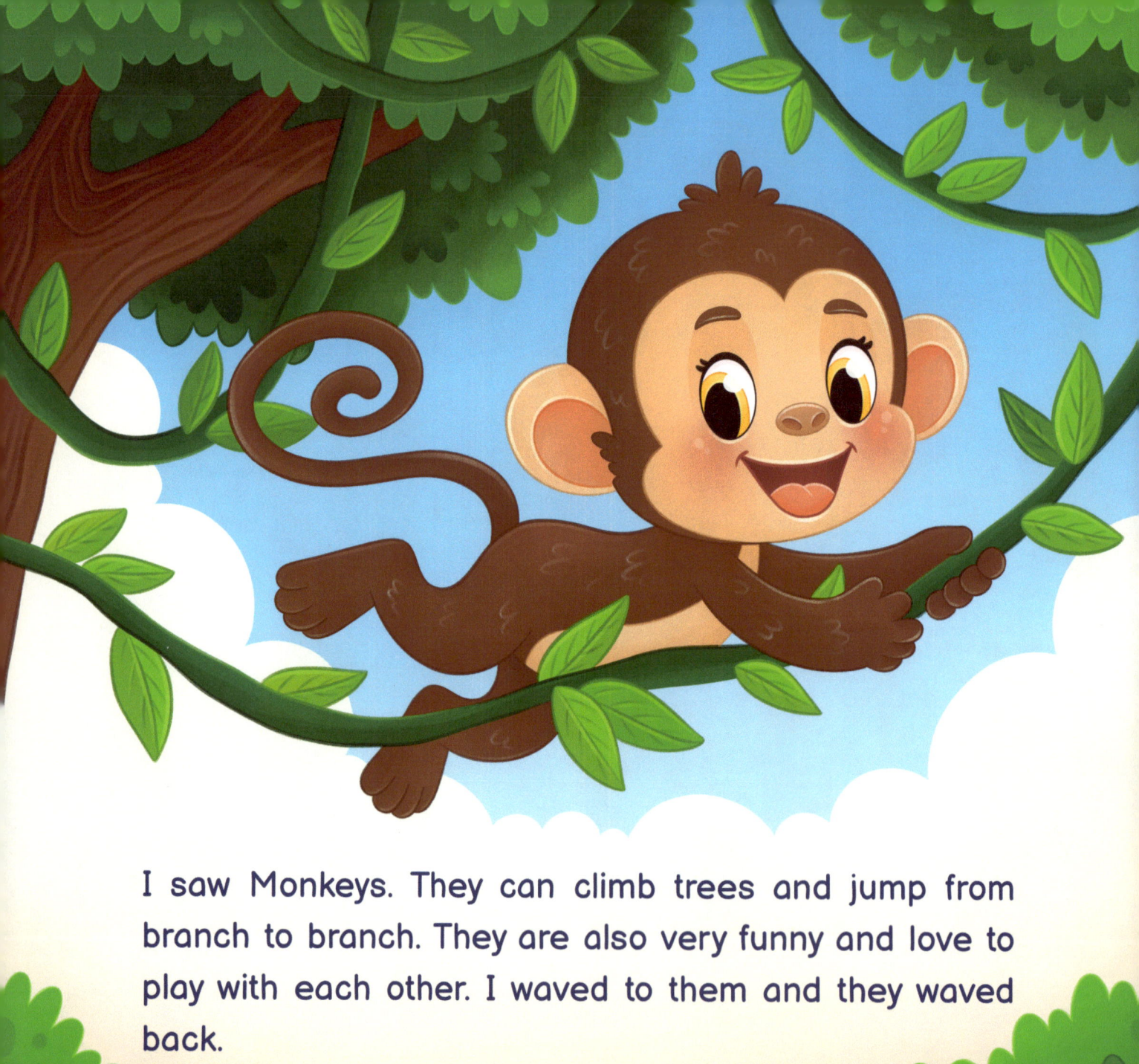

I saw Monkeys. They can climb trees and jump from branch to branch. They are also very funny and love to play with each other. I waved to them and they waved back.

I saw a Zebra and a Parrot. The Zebra has white and black stripes. She loves to run fast. And the Parrot has a big beak and can talk. He said "Hello!" to me. And I told him "Hello!" back.

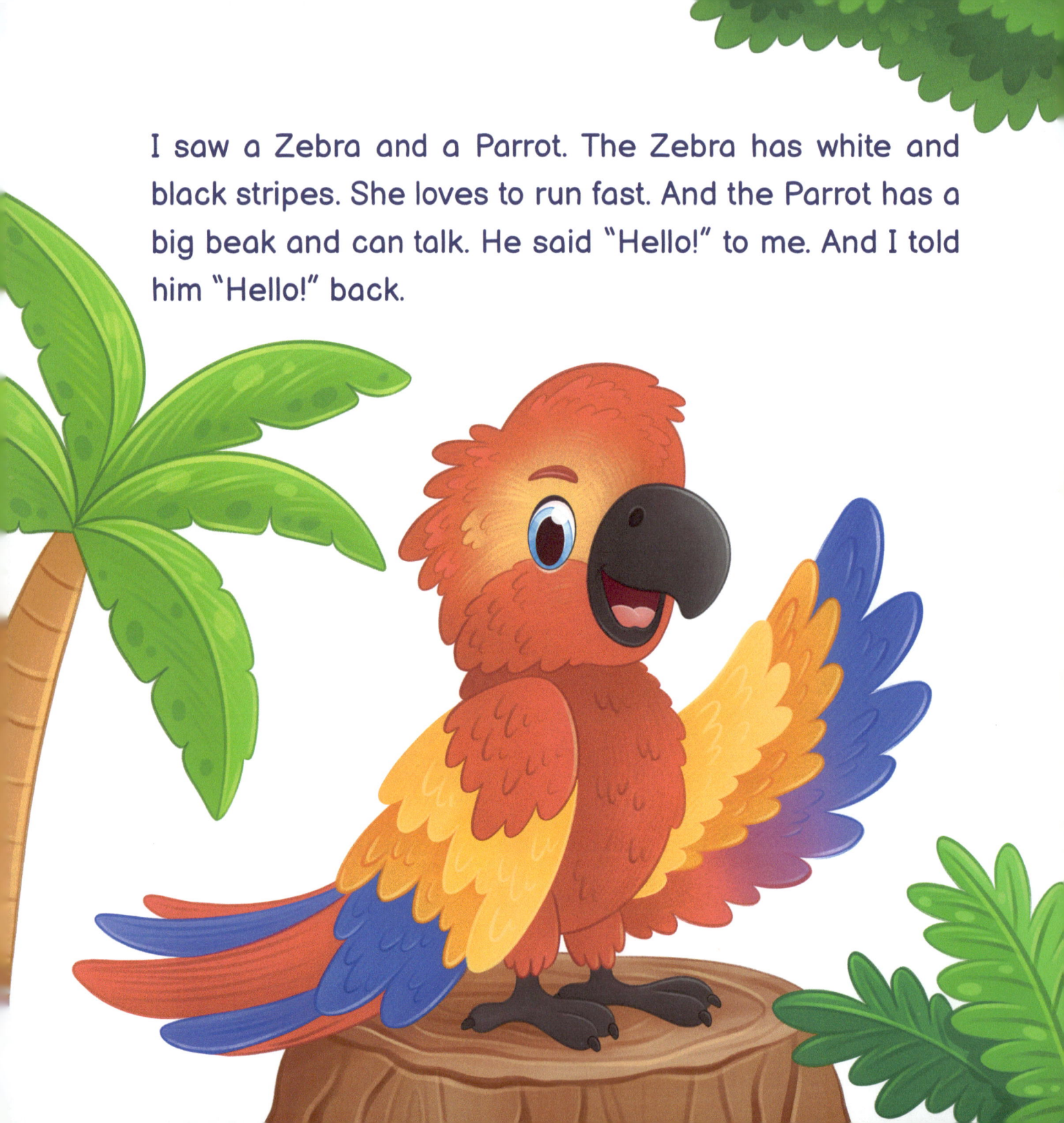

I really enjoyed the zoo. It was so interesting and fun! I want to go back again on the weekend to see the wonderful animals!

And now it's time for me to go home. When we see each other again, I'll tell you another great story. Bye!

A new day is here!

Do you remember Little Max?

Let's look for him and ask:
"Where have you been, Little Max?"

I went to the beach!

What is the beach?

A beach is a place with a lot of sand. And next to it there is a lot, a lot of water. This water is called the ocean. The ocean is so big that no matter how hard I tried, I couldn't see where it ended. Can you imagine?! And there are also waves and seagulls!

What were you doing at the Beach, Little Max?

I did all kinds of things! I took a bucket and shovel with me and built a sand castle. It came out well! Even Dolphins came around to see my work. They were very kind and funny!

I also saw Crabs and a Turtle. The Crabs were funny and looked important! They have eyes on thin rods and claws that look like large scissors. Crabs can cut down grass with their claws.

The Turtle was big, slow, and kind. Do you know that she carries her house with her? It's called a shell, and she can hide in it whenever she wants.

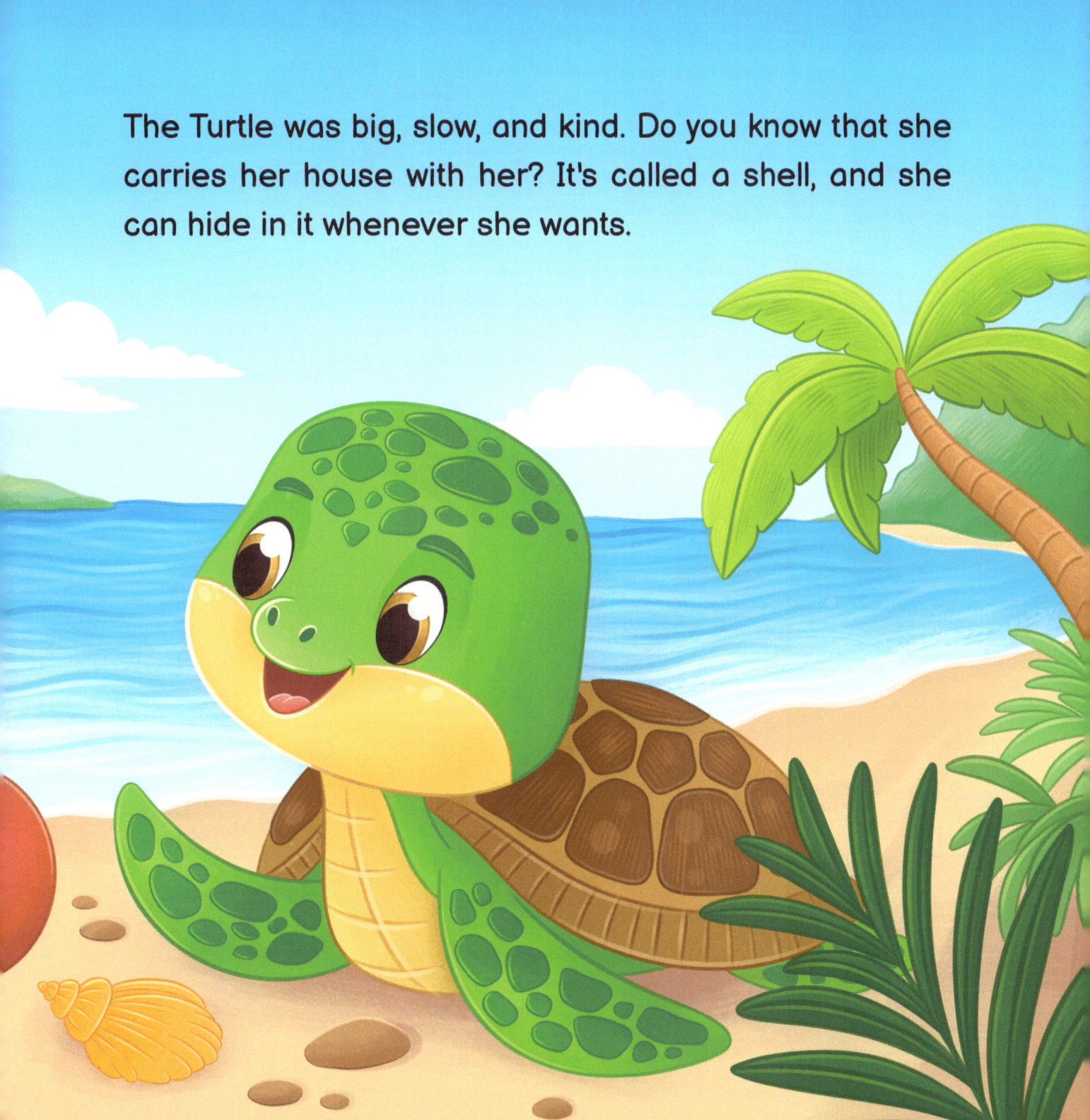

I also saw a huge white steamer with a chimney sailing on the ocean. I said hello to it, and it whistled to me like this: "Toot-toot!"

That was great! I didn't know that steamships said hello this way.

Steamboats are the most beautiful things in the world!
When I grow up, I will become a sailor, sail to different
countries and learn a lot of new things.

Also, for some reason, everyone loves to lay in the sun on the beach. I also lay down, but for just a bit. Sitting in one spot was boring. I ran off to play with the waves! The waves were catching up with me, and I was running away from them. It was fun!

There are beautiful shells and pebbles on the beach. You can collect them and take them home. I collected a whole lot. You know, if you put a shell to your ear, you can hear the sound of the ocean. It's true! I keep the shells and pebbles in my room now, so I can play with them and remember what a great time I had at the beach!

Well, it's time for me to run on. See you! When we see each other again, I'll tell you another fun story! Bye!

A new day is here!

Let's call Little Max and ask him:
"Where have you been, Little Max?"

I was at the fair!

What is a fair, little Max?

The fair is the most amazing place in the world! You can play, get gifts, have all sorts of delicious treats, and even ride a real horse! And the music is playing all the time!

What were you doing at the fair, little Max?

I rode on this big wheel. It's called the Ferris Wheel. The wheel takes you really high up, and you can see everything around you!

I also ate cotton candy, a caramel apple, and the most delicious cookies ever!

Then I rode a small horse. She was so cute and had a very funny snort. I told her "Thank you!" and she waved her head at me.

I also saw a real clown! He greeted me and gave me a balloon. He had red hair. He was cheerful and spoke in a funny voice. I became very good friends with him.

Then I had to throw a ball inside a ring. I threw and missed. But they still gave me a little toy car! Can you imagine?! Wow! Being at the fair is just so much fun!

There was also a real orchestra there. Musicians were wearing cool hats and had different instruments. They played various melodies, and they also allowed me to play their largest instrument. It's called a drum. It is so loud that you can hear it from far, far away!

Well, that's it for now. It's time for me to run along. When we see each other again, I will tell you another exciting story! Goodbye!

A new day is here!

It's time for another fun story about Little Max!

Let's call him and ask:
Where have you been, Little Max?

I went on a picnic.

What is a picnic, Little Max?

A picnic is when you go on a short nature trip to eat, play and have fun in a beautiful place.

You need to take a basket, put delicious food inside it and go to the park. Then spread a blanket on the grass and have a real feast!

The park is so beautiful! There's lots of different trees, flowers and birds. There are even squirrels there! They are very curious animals! The squirrels sat in the tree and watched me blow bubbles. They really liked the bubbles! I wanted to treat the squirrels to some cookies, but they ran away. The next time I see them, we will definitely become friends!

There was also a children's playground in the park. I rode on the swings and went down the big slide! It was a lot of fun!

After that I decided to rest a little. I just sat on the blanket and looked at the sky. There were clouds up there that looked like white sheep!

Picnics are fun! I want to go to the park again and make friends with the squirrels!

It's time for me to go! See you soon! Bye!

Where have you been, Little Max?
Magic of Discoveries Series

Published by Magic of Discoveries LLC.
For permissions contact: magicofdiscoveries@gmail.com
ISBN: 978-1-963328-58-5
First printing edition 2024

Disclaimer and Terms of Use:
The author and the publisher do not hold any responsibility for errors, omissions or contrary interpretation of the subject matter herein.

This book is presented solely for motivational and informational purposes only.

ALSO IN THE COLLECTION

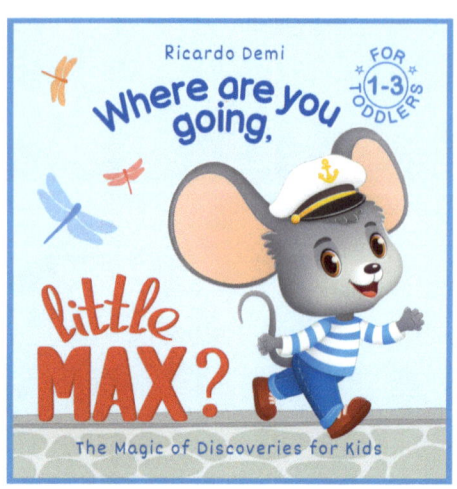

www.ingramcontent.com/pod-product-compliance
Lightning Source LLC
Chambersburg PA
CBHW040959170626
46815CB00002B/73